Follow That Ghost!

Follow That Ghost!

by Dale Fife

illustrated by Joan Drescher

FIFE

A Unicorn Book
E. P. DUTTON   NEW YORK

Library of Congress Cataloging in Publication Data

Fife, Dale.   Follow that ghost!

(A Unicorn Book)
SUMMARY: Two amateur sleuths try to locate the source
of mysterious nocturnal tapping.
[1. Mystery and detective stories]
I. Drescher, Joan E.   II. Title.
PZ7.F4793Fo   Fic   79-11370   ISBN: 0-525-30010-4

Published in the United States by E. P. Dutton, a Division
of Sequoia-Elsevier Publishing Company, Inc., New York

Published simultaneously in Canada by Clarke,
Irwin & Company Limited, Toronto and Vancouver

Editor: Emilie McLeod   Designer: Stacie Rogoff

Printed in the U.S.A.   First Edition
10 9 8 7 6 5 4 3 2 1

To
Lynn, Marc, and Matthew
Carpenter

1

My name is Chuck. Jason is my best friend. He lives in the apartment below me. We have a Following Service. I have a notebook and a periscope from my detective set. Jason has a spyglass. We both have flashlights.

Nobody has hired us yet. But we practice.

Today we are following Glory. She lives in the apartment house next door. It's the only house on the street with a tree. Glory is

easy to follow because she carries a cello on the way to her music lesson.

Glory crosses the street. We hide behind a car for a moment. We run after her. Our sneakers make no noise.

But at the vacant lot Glory stops. She whirls around.

"Why are you following me?" she demands.

"It's our business," I say. "We follow people and find out things."

"You aren't very good at it," she says.

"We're just practicing," Jason says, with his mouth full of peanuts.

"We need a real case," I say.

"Maybe I'll hire you," Glory says. "How much do you charge?"

Charge? Jason and I go into a huddle.

Jason doesn't talk much—unless it's about food. He likes peanuts best.

"Glory makes good fudge," Jason says. "She puts salty peanuts in it. We could

charge her four pieces of fudge a day—two for you and two for me—until we solve the case."

That is a long speech for Jason. I like fudge too. Jason and I shake hands on the deal.

But Glory shakes her head. "You solve the case first. Then I will give you a pan of fudge."

"What is the case?" I ask. "Who do we follow?"

"A ghost," Glory says. "It comes every morning around five o'clock. It wakes us up. It's scary. My mother can't sleep and she gets headaches. We don't want a ghost hanging around our apartment."

Glory sometimes exaggerates. "How do you know it is a ghost?" I ask.

"Because we hear it but can't see it. It knocks. It taps. It pounds on our walls. But nothing's there."

"I don't know if we can follow a ghost," I tell Glory.

"It's too weird," Jason says.

"If you're scared, forget it," Glory says. "If the ghost stays, my mother won't. She likes our apartment. It has lots of windows. We can see the oak tree and the birds. I don't want to move."

Our street needs Glory. No Glory, no salty peanut fudge.

I look at Jason. Jason looks at me.

"We'll try," I say.

2

Jason and I go to my apartment. In my room we write out the order:

FOLLOW GHOST FOR GLORY

We spear it onto our order spindle, which is a nail in a block of wood.

"How do we follow something we can't see?" Jason asks.

A good question.

"We need to get information on ghosts," I say.

"Let's go see Krink," Jason says. "She knows everything."

"A good idea," I say. Krink tells ghost stories.

Krink lives in the only single house on our block. It's old. Spooky. She answers the door in a skeleton costume even though Halloween is a long way off.

"What do you know about ghosts?" I ask.

"I know all about ghosts," Krink says.

"How do you follow a ghost?" Jason asks.

"That's impossible," Krink says. "The ghost follows you."

We believe her.

It is getting dark. On the way home, Jason and I keep looking back to see if a ghost is following us.

I see a cat running in front of us. The wind howls around the corners of buildings. Awnings rattle. Thunder rumbles. We start to run.

But when we reach the floor where my apartment is, Glory is in the hall waiting with samples of fudge. One piece for me—one for Jason.

"I'm sorry, Glory, we cannot accept your fudge," I say. "We can't follow a ghost."

Jason eyes his piece of fudge. He takes a nibble. Then another. He gobbles the whole piece. "I'll do anything for salty peanut fudge," he says.

Jason and I are partners. I eat my piece of salty peanut fudge very fast. "We'll try," I say.

"My mother is nervous," Glory says. "Please hurry and do something about the ghost so we don't have to move."

3

Jason and I worry about the case.

"Let's start by investigating the scene of the crime," I say.

"Where is it?" Jason asks.

"Glory's apartment house, of course."

I get out my notebook. I write:

> Glory's apartment—
> third floor—back windows

Jason cracks peanut shells. "Let's go," he says.

"We will wait until tonight," I say. "When the ghost starts knocking, we will be on the spot."

We get our parents' permission to put our sleeping bags under the tree next to Glory's apartment house.

We take Jason's flashlight.

It's dark. One by one the lights go out in the apartment house. We didn't know the dark would be so dark.

Jason munches peanuts. I tell jokes to keep awake—and so that we will not hear scary sounds.

We hear them anyhow. There is a loud *crunch-crunch*. A THING growls. A police siren comes close. It goes away. Something hops over our sleeping bags. The tree whispers in the wind. A pair of eyes blinks at us—*HOO! HOO! HOO!*—and we are out of our bags and on our feet. We race home, dragging all our stuff.

The next day we bump into Krink. "How's the case coming?" she asks.

"Not good," I admit.

She gives us advice. "Most ghosts live in-doors. They walk down halls and hide in closets. This is probably an inside job."

Inside Job. A good clue. I add it to my notebook.

Jason and I decide to make a door-to-door search of Glory's apartment house.

4

We begin at the bottom. Mr. Ivy lives in the basement apartment. He is an artist. While he is waiting to become famous, he does odd jobs around the apartment house. In his own apartment he paints pictures of trees. Big trees. Little trees. Forests of trees. The walls of his apartment are covered with trees.

He answers our knock wearing blue jeans and a paint-streaked shirt. Through the open

door everything looks dark. It might be a place for a ghost to hide.

"Have you heard the ghost that knocks on Glory's walls?" I ask.

"It does not come down to the basement," Mr. Ivy says in a hurry.

"The ghost scares Glory's mother," I say. "She is going to move unless we can get rid of it."

Mr. Ivy glances back at his apartment full of painted trees. "I'll be glad to make an exchange—her apartment for mine. Even a ghost would not like it down here." He slams the door.

Nobody is home on the first floor.

A friendly lady tells us about the people on her floor.

We walk past the baron's apartment, which is next door to Glory's. As usual, it has a Do Not Disturb sign on the doorknob. We don't disturb the baron. He is an important man with an accent.

We go to the top floor and knock on a

door. Mrs. Clacker pokes her head out. She laughs when we tell her about Glory's ghost. "Sounds like Glory," she says. "She is a prevaricator."

We wonder what a prevaricator is.

"Let's stop at Krink's," I say. "She has a big dictionary. Besides, we can ask her more about ghosts."

5

Krink comes to the door wearing a sheet over her jeans.

We borrow her dictionary and she helps us find *prevaricator*. The three of us agree that Glory is not a prevaricator. Maybe not always quite truthful, but not a liar.

"We must find a way to help Glory," I say. "We must get rid of the ghost."

"I've read lots of books about ghosts," Krink says. "I know exactly what to do."

"What?" Jason asks.

"We must coax the ghost out of Glory's apartment house and bury it," Krink says.

"How do you bury a ghost?" I ask.

"You and Jason dig a grave," Krink says. "I will bring my magic candle and say the secret words that call a ghost. Then, real quick, I'll grab it and stuff it in the grave. You cover it up. It will never rise again."

"Where do we dig a grave? In my father's window box?" Jason asks.

Krink shakes her head. "The ghost needs room."

"How about the vacant lot across the street from Glory's apartment house?" I say. "The bulldozer plowed up the ground."

"So it's easy to dig," Jason says.

Until a few weeks ago the lot had high weeds, some old dead trees, and a tumble-down shack that Krink said was haunted.

"A great idea, Chuck," says Krink. "I

think the ghost that pesters Glory and her mother used to live in that shack, and now it has no place to go."

"Then we'd better hurry and give it a place," I say.

"Let's go," Jason says.

"We'll have to wait until it's dark," Krink says.

I don't like the idea. I don't think Jason does either, the way he is stuffing peanuts into his mouth. But business is business.

6

We dig a two-foot hole with our hands and an old license plate while Krink holds her magic candle stub.

Krink squeezes her eyes shut. She sways from side to side. She chants:

> Wibbledy wobbledy
> Bumpety bump
> We have dug your grave
> With a clumpety clump.

A cold wind snakes around us. It blows

out the candle. I feel goose bumps. I hear Jason crunching peanuts.

Krink points at something in the air. "I see it," she yells. "The ghost!"

I'm almost too scared to look. I turn toward Krink. I see moving shadows and Krink shoving something invisible into the grave.

Her voice is deep and hollow:

> Rattledy rattle
> Thumpety thump
> We'll cover you over
> With a humpety hump.

"Cover it over," Krink orders.

My hands refuse to move. They feel frozen.

"HURRY," Krink says. "Do it right, or the ghost will rise again."

She doesn't need to tell me to hurry. I can't see what we're covering over, but I help Jason throw in the dirt at top speed.

We are all up and running. My feet feel

buried in glue. They want to stay in one spot. I think I'll never reach the street.

We stop to catch our breath under the streetlight.

"The ghost is gone forevermore," Krink says.

We rush up the apartment stairs to tell Glory.

"We have buried your ghost," I tell her.

"We have come for the salty peanut fudge," Jason says.

Glory's smile shows all her teeth. "I'll make the fudge tonight and bring it to you first thing in the morning."

We feel good walking home.

Jason and I have solved our first case. We talk about our great success.

We talk about the big pan of salty peanut fudge which Glory will give us tomorrow.

Glory comes around early the next morning. Jason and I are waiting. Glory does not have the fudge. She is not smiling.

"I made the fudge and I'm going to eat it

all myself," she says. "The ghost was noisier than ever this morning. My mother is very upset. She's going apartment hunting today."

This is serious. Yesterday we had a satisfied customer. Today we don't.

While Jason grinds away noisily on peanuts, I sit down and think.

"Jason, what knocks besides a ghost?" I ask.

"People?" Jason says.

PEOPLE!

"But we have overlooked one thing, Jason."

"What?"

"MOTIVE! Every crime has a motive. A reason."

"What would be the reason for scaring Glory and her mother?" Jason asks.

"Someone might want their apartment," I say.

"Who?" Jason asks.

"That's for us to find out. First we will have to look at the names of the people in the apartment house."

7

The only stranger to us in Glory's apartment house is the baron. No one knows him. We don't know if he is a real baron, but he looks like one. He has a pointed beard and bushy eyebrows. Every noon he leaves the apartment house carrying a suitcase.

Jason and I wonder what he carries in the suitcase.

"We could ask him," Jason says.

Jason knows better. You can't ask a baron

who wears gold braid on his jacket a question like that.

We ask Mrs. Clacker instead.

Mrs. Clacker winks. "The baron has international ties."

Jason and I try to figure that out.

"Maybe he's a smuggler," Jason says.

"Or a spy," I say. "SPY! An international spy who taps out messages—dots . . . dashes—the MORSE CODE! And that's the noise that scares Glory's mother."

"But why does he do it on Glory's wall?" asks Jason, spilling peanut shells on the floor.

"We must follow the baron," I say. "Find out where he goes—who he sees."

"If he's a spy it might be dangerous," Jason says.

"Business is business," I tell him.

We plan our strategy.

"He travels by motorbike," I say.

"Hard to follow," Jason says. "We do not even have bicycles."

"We'll have to use our skateboards," I say.
Following a motorbike is not easy. It is almost impossible on skateboards, especially
since I am carrying my periscope and Jason
has a bag of peanut butter sandwiches.

We are in the BIG CHASE. We careen through streets, roar around corners. People scatter. Dogs bark. Cats climb trees.

The baron makes a quick turn into a square with people and tables. We are close behind. Too close.

Jason runs into the baron. I run into Jason. We are in a heap. The baron's suitcase bursts open. Things spill out. Jason's

lunch bag hits a table. It rains peanut butter
sandwiches.

We are terrified. Trapped in a nest of
spies. We might be captured—tortured.

While the baron sits there rubbing one
leg, we roll away under a table. I use my
periscope to see what's happening. The baron
is shaking his head. He does not know what
ran into him. He gets to his feet.

I look around at the tables. "It's a FLEA MARKET," I say.

We creep out a little to watch the baron. He is scooping up the contents of his suitcase. He puts the things on a table. We see ties—checkered ties, striped ties, plaid ties, polka-dotted ties—ties, ties, ties.

The baron hangs up a sign:

Buy Authentic International
Neckties from the Baron!

Jason and I look at each other in disgust. We sneak away.

We cross the baron's name off our suspect list and head for home.

8

On our street we bump into Glory and her mother. They are carrying empty cardboard boxes.

Glory looks sad. "We're giving notice that we're going to move. I'll be packing up the sugar and the cocoa and the salty peanuts."

Glory's mother looks sad too. "I'll miss the sun and the tree and the birds," she says. "I'm sorry you two detectives didn't solve the mystery."

We're sorry too. Jason crams his mouth with peanuts. I do the same.

"Did you hear what Glory's mother called us?" Jason asks in a crunchy voice. "Detectives."

"They never give up on a case," I say. "They keep hunting for clues. Maybe we don't have the proper equipment."

"I still have my father's magnifying glass and my false mustache from Halloween," Jason says.

"I have binoculars," I say.

We rush home to find these things. Then we rush back to Glory's apartment house.

Mr. Ivy is perched on a ladder. He is painting the No Vacancy sign. We are sure he will not know us in our raincoats. But right away he shouts down at us: "Have you found the ghost?"

"We're looking for clues," I shout back.

While I cover every inch of the apartment building with my binoculars, Jason searches

the ground with his magnifying glass. "I found a clue," he yells. "Look at these shells."

"Peanut shells," I say. "You are supposed to FIND evidence, not make it."

Suddenly, through my binoculars, I see something I have not noticed before—a small hole several feet above one of the windows of Glory's apartment. I see a second hole—a third—a long string of holes.

We are onto something. But what?

"Who could reach that high?" I ask.

"No human," Jason says. "It's got to be a ghost."

"Can a ghost make holes?" I ask.

Just then Mr. Ivy comes around the side of the apartment house. He is carrying a ladder over his shoulder. It is a tall ladder. When he gets below Glory's bedroom window, he stands and looks up.

I look at Jason. He looks at me.

"Mr. Ivy has a motive," I say. "He does not like the basement. He likes trees. He likes Glory's apartment."

"It can't be Mr. Ivy. He's a nice man," Jason says. "I still think we're looking for a ghost."

"Circumstantial evidence points to Mr. Ivy," I argue.

We decide there is just one way to settle this. We will sleep under the tree again. This time we'll stay all night.

9

We bring an alarm clock and flashlights and our sleeping bags. This time we set the alarm clock for exactly four-thirty. We do not tell jokes. We listen. We hear a grunt and a whistle.

"What's that?" Jason whispers.

"Someone snoring," I whisper back.

Footsteps crunch nearby. Something brushes Jason's face. "The ghost," he yells.

I flip on my flashlight. Nothing's there. We laugh—sort of.

Something icy hits our heads. We sit bolt upright. A splash of rain. We creep down low in our sleeping bags. We cover our heads.

I don't wake up until the alarm clock rings. I punch Jason. He growls. "Shssh—watch," I say.

It's not easy to keep your eyes open so early in the morning. But business is business.

Minutes tick away. We watch.

FIVE O'CLOCK!

A shadow moves around the corner of the house.

Jason grabs my arm. "The ghost," he whispers.

It comes closer. It is all white. It steals along the side of the apartment house. It turns. We see its face. IT IS MR. IVY. In pajamas. He peers all around. He looks up at Glory's window. He scrunches on all fours. He starts to creep under a bush.

Jason and I are on our feet. We make a flying tackle and land on Mr. Ivy's back.

"HELP! MURDER!" he yelps.

He is a little man, but he has a big voice.

Windows open.

People shout.

The baron blows a shrill alarm whistle.

Glory's mother yells.

Glory yells.

A police siren winds down in front of the apartment. Two officers rush towards us.

Glory and her mother come running, bathrobes flying.

Krink, wrapped in a blanket, comes rushing.

"Here's your ghost," I say to Glory's mother.

"We caught him red-handed," Jason says.

Jason and I are pleased with ourselves.

Glory's mother yanks Jason and me away from Mr. Ivy. "I hired this man to watch my apartment," she says.

The baron slams down his window.

Glory scowls at us. The police grin and roar away.

We feel terrible. We like Mr. Ivy. He sits under the bush shaking his head.

Glory's mother pats his shoulder. "I'm sorry. Maybe I'll buy one of your paintings," she says.

Glory drops to the grass next to Mr. Ivy. "Now we'll really have to move," she says. "I'll miss all my friends. I'll miss you too."

Krink flops down beside her. "The street won't be the same without you."

Glory's mother sighs and looks up into the tree. "I like this tree. I like our apartment. But I don't like the strange noises I've been hearing."

Jason and I look at each other. We are failures. If we had solved the case, everyone here would be happy. Now everyone is sad. Jason cracks peanuts as fast as he can. I sit on a limb of the tree and I think about running away. Far off somewhere where no one knows me.

And then—I hear a sharp *tap-tap-tap*. It's coming from the apartment house. I look up above Glory's window. "THE GHOST!" I yell and catapult out of the tree.

"WHERE?" Jason shouts, jumping to his feet.

But now it's gone.

"I saw it. Over Glory's window. It's black and white and has red on his head."

"I heard it too," Glory's mother says. "The same noise I've heard every morning."

Krink draws her blanket around her. "Everybody be quiet. Maybe it will come back."

And then it does. "Look," I whisper.

"THAT WOODPECKER," Jason says. "You mean it is the noisy ghost?"

"Listen," I say. With its beak the woodpecker is banging at the wood like a hammer:

KNOCK-KNOCK-KNOCK-KNOCK

Now its mate joins him:

KNOCKKNOCKKNOCKKNOCKKNOCK

The children fly in:

knock knock knock knock

Glory's mother watches, open-mouthed. "And THIS is what we've been hearing."

It's hard for Krink to give up the ghost theory. "Do you mean to say that there never was a ghost?"

"Right," I say. "It was the woodpecker family all along."

"I get it," Jason says. "When the lot was cleared, the woodpeckers lost their home."

"Precisely," I say, as the detectives do on TV. "They had to find a new home, and a new place to get their food."

"They won't stay here long," Mr. Ivy says. "They're like me—they like trees, trees, trees. As soon as they find a woodsy place, they'll travel on."

Glory bounces to her feet. "Now we won't ever have to move."

She gives everyone a hug and races off.

We all begin to laugh. Glory's mother laughs hardest of all.

When Glory comes back, she has a pan of salty peanut fudge. Jason and I feel good. I pass it around. Everyone is chomping and smiling.

Jason and I chomp fudge all the way
home.

In my room we take Glory's order off the spindle. In big letters we write on it:

1